My Auntie's Shoes

Amanda S McKay

Illustrated by: Joshua Allen

AuthorHouse™
1663 Liberty Drive
Bloomington, IN 47403
www.authorhouse.com
Phone: 1-800-839-8640

First published by AuthorHouse 10/12/2011

ISBN: 978-1-4567-9558-0 (sc)

Library of Congress Control Number: 2011915232

Printed in the United States of America

Any people depicted in stock imagery provided by Thinkstock are models,
and such images are being used for illustrative purposes only.
Certain stock imagery © Thinkstock.

This book is printed on acid-free paper.

To Ally, who keeps my heart light.

My name is Ally.
I am two!
And I love, I love, my auntie's shoes,
Her Vera Wangs and Jimmy Choos.
Oh, yes I do,
I love, I love, my auntie's shoes.

Some are shiny.
Some are flat.
Some are blacker than my cat.

Shoes with sparkles,
Shoes with bows
All line up in nice, neat rows.

There's nothing I can do.
I love, I love, my auntie's shoes.

So up the hallway I will sneak
Just so I can take a peek
And just maybe try them on my feet.

Shoes with buckles,
Shoes with feathers,
Shoes with soft Italian leather.

Oh yes, it's true!
I love, I love, my auntie's shoes.

So when the coast is finally clear,
I quickly find my favorite pair,
And in the mirror I stop to stare
At the princess now standing there.

I start to dance like I am at a ball
when I hear my auntie call,
"Ally Jean Audrey Beaton McKay,
Take off my shoes!"

My name is Ally.
I am two.
And my auntie doesn't like it when I play
in her shoes.

CPSIA information can be obtained
at www.ICGtesting.com
Printed in the USA
257007LV00001B